## Hidenori Kusaka

I've completed my Galar Pokédex! It took a long time to capture 400 types of Pokémon, but it was worth it! I know you'll have a great time playing too!

## Satoshi Yamamoto

What I like best about *Pokémon: Sword/Shield*:
① How the music changes during the battle when Pokémon go Dynamax! When the chorus kicks in, it's really exciting!

# Pokémon™ Sword & Shield

## 1

STORY
**Hidenori Kusaka**

ART
**Satoshi Yamamoto**

## Henry
# SWORD

HENRY IS A CRAFTSMAN WHO UNDERSTANDS POKÉMON GEAR. HE IS THE DESCENDANT OF A RENOWNED SWORDSMITH AND USES FAMILY SECRETS TO ENHANCE THE GEAR HE COMES ACROSS.

## Casey
# SHIELD

CASEY IS AN ACE COMPUTER HACKER WHO CAN CRACK ANY CODE AND GUESS ANY PASSWORD. SHE'S PROFESSOR MAGNOLIA'S ASSISTANT AND CHIPS IN AS THE TEAM'S DATA ANALYST.

# Character Introduction

## Marvin

MARVIN'S A ROOKIE TRAINER WHO RECENTLY MOVED TO GALAR. HE'S EXCITED TO LEARN EVERYTHING HE CAN ABOUT POKÉMON!

## Professor Magnolia

## Leon

LEON IS THE BEST TRAINER IN GALAR. HE'S THE UNDEFEATED CHAMPION!

## Sonia

SONIA IS PROFESSOR MAGNOLIA'S GRANDDAUGHTER AND LEON'S CHILDHOOD FRIEND. SHE SETS OUT TO INVESTIGATE THE GALAR REGION LEGEND AFTER BEING PROMPTED TO DO SO BY PROFESSOR MAGNOLIA.

# CONTENTS

WHAT? A ZIG-ZAGOON ?!
IT'S A ZIG-ZAGOON ?!
I HEARD THE GALAR REGION'S POKÉMON WERE A LITTLE DIFFERENT FROM THOSE IN OTHER REGIONS...
...BUT THEY'RE REALLY DIFFER-ENT!
ZIG
ZIG
ZIG
!
ZIG
ZIG

Adventure 1 Wow!! That's One Big Pokémon...

IT DISAP-PEARED?
SHWOO...
WOW! ARE ALL GALAR PANGORO SO HUGE?!
AAAHH !!
THUNK
OOF.
HEY!

YOU OKAY?
I'LL GET YOU DOWN IN A JIFFY.
CARE TO LEND A WING?
FWOOSH
FWUMP

TAP
YOU SAVED MY LIFE!
AND YOU ARE...?
IT'S A POKÉMON CALLED SIRFETCH'D!
SO, HOW ARE YOU FEELING?
I'M OKAY.
BUT...
UH...
UMM...

EEK!
SHA
WHAAAAAAAAAT?!
DASH

SUR-PRISED?
BOO!
HEY!
WERE YOU SURPRISED OR NOT?!
STOMP STOMP
WELL?!
DON'T TEASE HIM!
CASEY SHIELD! THIS BOY HAS JUST HAD A HUGE SCARE.

IS IT SCARY? I THINK BALL GUY LOOKS CUTE.
THAT'S NOT THE POINT...
SO, WHAT'S YOUR NAME?
I'M MARVIN.
MARVIN, EH?
WE WERE JUST ABOUT TO MAKE CAMP...
...WHEN YOU FELL OFF THAT CLIFF, SCREAMING.
SO WHAT HAPPENED?
WERE YOU TESTING YOUR COURAGE? OR DID A BULLY DARE YOU TO JUMP? I KNOW, A SCARY POKÉMON WAS CHASING YOU AROUND AND...!
CASEY, HUSH!
NO!
THERE WAS A HUGE PANGORO! THEN IT DISAP-PEARED...
...SO I WENT OVER TO THE CLIFF TO GET A CLOSER LOOK...
...

DON'T CALL ME MARV...
AND WHAT DO YOU MEAN?
MY BAD, MARV!
THIS IS ALL YOUR FAULT, CASEY.
OOPSY!
SHIELD, SLOW DOWN!
SCREEECH
WHAT I MEAN IS I WAS TESTING OUT MY DYNAMAX SIMULATOR BECAUSE PEOPLE HARDLY COME HERE, SO I THOUGHT IT'D BE FINE! I MADE THE DYNAMAX SIMULATOR MYSELF—IT'S A HOLOGRAM, A STEREOSCOPIC IMAGE! PRETTY AMAZING, HUH?! I MADE IT LOOK LIKE A HUGE POKÉMON, BUT ACTUALLY...
BUT YOU HAVE TO BE QUIET! DON'T RAISE YOUR VOICE, OKAY?!
THIS WAY!
OH SURE!
I THINK IT'S TIME TO THANK THE PERSON AND THE POKÉMON WHO SAVED ME...

HENRY, IT'S ME!
MARVIN WANTED TO THANK YOU AND SIRFETCH'D!!
THIS IS QUIET?!
WHAT?

HEY, HENRY!
IS THIS THE SAME GUY?
YES. THANK YOU VERY MUCH FOR SAVING ME.
HEY, MARVIN! ARE YOU ALL RIGHT?
SORRY, CASEY! WHEN DID YOU COME IN?
I WAS FIXING SIR-FETCH'D'S LEEK SPEAR.
SO WHAT WERE YOU DOING?
HENRY, YOU'RE CONCEN-TRATING TOO HARD!

HENRY IS A GEAR CRAFTSMAN.
GEAR?
FARFETCH'D'S SPEAR, MAROWAK'S BONE, SAMUROTT'S SEAMITAR, DELPHOX'S WAND, GURDURR'S STEEL BEAM...
THAT'S ALL GEAR—OR AT LEAST THAT'S WHAT SWORD CALLS IT.
I HAVE TO CALL IT SOMETHING...
GEAR IS WHAT YOU CALL THE TOOLS POKÉMON USE IN THEIR DAILY LIVES AND BATTLES.
BUT THEY SUFFER FROM WEAR AND TEAR, LIKE ANYTHING ELSE.
MY JOB IS TO KEEP THEM IN PERFECT CONDITION.
GROOKEY, COME HERE.
THIS IS THE CHIMP POKÉMON, GROOKEY.
THE STICK IT'S HOLDING IS A PIECE OF GEAR TOO.
IF I DO THIS...
SHFF
THE STICK BECOMES HARDER AND STRONGER.
HUH!

THAT MAKES SENSE! SOUND GOOD, MARVIN?
USE THE VR DECK. IF YOU SURPRISE SOMEONE ELSE, YOU MIGHT CAUSE ANOTHER ACCIDENT.
NOW COME SEE MY DYNAMAX SIMULATOR!
HOLD IT, CASEY.
MAYBE TELL ME WHAT THE DYNAMAX SIMULATOR IS FIRST?
FIRST THINGS FIRST—THE VR DECK!
ONCE YOU'RE JACKED INTO THE SIMULATOR, YOU'LL UNDER-STAND EVERY-THING!
SWIP
TRY AND KEEP UP, MARV!
I JUST MOVED HERE, SO I DON'T KNOW ANYTHING ABOUT THIS REGION.
WHOA!

OH WOW!
GREAT, NOW LET'S FIGHT! I'LL USE MY SCORBUNNY! YOU DON'T HAVE A POKÉMON, DO YOU, MARVIN?
YOU CAN FIGHT WITH MY SIRFETCH'D.
UM... WAIT A MINUTE!

I BARELY KNOW EITHER OF YOU!
I DON'T EVEN KNOW YOUR FULL NAMES!
OH! I'M HENRY SWORD.
CALL ME HENRY OR SWORD OR WHATEVER YOU LIKE.
I'M CASEY SHIELD.
I GUESS YOU COULD CALL ME JUST SHIELD, BUT IT'S PER-FECTLY FINE TO CALL ME JUST CASEY!
I'M PROFESSOR MAGNOLIA.
I DON'T THINK WE NEED TO BE ON A FIRST-NAME BASIS, YOUNG MAN.
OF COURSE, PROFES-SOR!
THAT'S TOO MANY NAMES ANYWAY!

THE SECRETS OF DYNAMAX, PART 1

▲Professor Magnolia's research is still ongoing.

**Professor Magnolia**

The Pokémon of Galar can become enormous by Dynamaxing. Professor Magnolia discovered the amazing scientific process behind this regional phenomenon ten years ago.

## Adventure 2 Crackle!! Practice Battle

ALL RIGHT.
SO...
HENRY SWORD...
...AND CASEY SHIELD ...
...AND PROFES-SOR MAGNOLIA.
NOW PUT ON THE VR DECK ALREADY!
LET'S GET YOU JACKED INTO THE SIMULA-TOR.
AUGH!

SWOOP...
CASEY, WE NEED TO WEAR THEM TOO.
WELL, DUH!
YOU TOO, EVERYONE!
BUT I'VE NEVER HAD A POKÉMON BATTLE BEFORE!
SERIOUSLY?!
READY, MARVIN?
READY FOR WHAT?
TO DEFEAT THIS PANGORO IN A POKÉMON BATTLE, OF COURSE!
I KNOW THE THEORY!
EVERY POKÉMON HAS SPECIAL MOVES THAT WEAKEN THEIR OPPONENT.
IF A TRAINER WANTS TO CAPTURE THAT POKÉMON, THEY MUST THROW A POKÉ BALL BEFORE THE POKÉMON IS UNABLE TO BATTLE.

OKAY.
BOOT IT UP, PROFES-SOR!
LET'S TRY TOGETHER.
THAT'S RIGHT!
GWOOSH
AIEEE!
THUNGK!
WHAT ?!
THOSE WERE HIGH FREQUENCY ELECTRIC WAVES! I THOUGHT IT WOULD BE A MORE REALISTIC EXPERIENCE IF YOU FELT THE ATTACK. DON'T WORRY, YOU WON'T DIE IF YOU'RE HIT! TRUE, IT DOES HURT, SO THE SHOCK MIGHT...
THAT STUNG!
HEY, WHERE ARE YOU GOING?

PROFES-SOR, COULD YOU PAUSE THE BATTLE?
HALT...
MARVIN, WHY DO YOU KNOW THE RULES OF A POKÉMON BATTLE?
AND WHY DIDN'T YOU RUN AWAY WHEN YOU SAW THAT HUGE PANGORO?
ONE DAY, I WANT TO CATCH MY OWN POKÉMON, AND GO ON A JOURNEY...
...AND TRAIN IN THE POKÉMON GYMS TOO!
THEN YOU NEED TO PRACTICE!
GYM BATTLES IN GALAR ARE DYNAMAX BATTLES!
RESTART, PROFES-SOR!
BWOOSH!!

GROOKEY, USE LEAFAGE!
SCORBUNNY, USE EMBER!
CHOOM
CHOOM
KRRSHAA
SHUK SHUK SHUK SHUK
LOOK CLOSELY.
THERE IS ALWAYS A PAUSE BETWEEN THE ATTACK AND DEFENSE.
THAT'S TO PREPARE THE POKÉMON'S NEXT MOVES.
I LEARNED ABOUT IT AT THE TRAINERS' SCHOOL.
THEN YOU MAKE YOUR NEXT ATTACK.
AND YOU KEEP DOING THAT UNTIL YOU WIN!
AND THEN THERE'S TYPE ADVANTAGES TO CONSIDER.

PANGORO IS A DARK TYPE.
SIRFETCH'D IS A FIGHTING TYPE. IT CAN USE A MOVE CALLED METEOR ASSAULT.
THEN I'M AT AN ADVANTAGE WITH THE TYPE!
THAT WON'T BE ENOUGH!
WHEN POKÉMON DYNAMAX, THEY'RE TOUGHER, AND THEIR MOVES ARE STRONGER.
IF YOU KEEP YOUR DISTANCE, YOU'LL BECOME AN EASY TARGET.
YOU NEED TO HAVE THE COURAGE TO RUSH UP TO IT.
GULP...
GO ON.
PAP
AHHHHHHH!

IT REALLY HURTS!
OW!!
THUNK
POKÉMON BATTLES ARE SCARY!
I DON'T WANT TO DO THIS!
SIR-FETCH'D ...
...!
THE PAUSE!

SIR-
FETCH'D!
IT'S
TIME!
METEOR
ASSAULT!!
SHH
SSSH!!

SIRFETCH'D PROTECTED ME...
YOUR TIMING WAS PERFECT.
YOU DID IT, MARV!
BUT I COULDN'T FIT INTO THE SCHOOL IN GALAR...
I WAS AN HONORS STUDENT AT THE TRAINERS' SCHOOL IN MY PREVIOUS REGION.
A PARTNERSHIP WITH A POKÉMON...
BUT NOW...
THAT'S WHY I HAVEN'T BEEN GOING TO SCHOOL. AND I DIDN'T HAVE THE COURAGE TO SET OUT ON MY OWN JOURNEY...
I LEARNED ABOUT IT AT SCHOOL, BUT THIS IS THE REAL THING...
...I CAN'T WAIT TO SET OUT!

WE CAN DO THAT ON THE WAY!
I SHOULD PROBABLY TELL MY PARENTS...
THEN COME WITH US!
WHAT?
YOU DON'T MIND, DO YOU, PROFESSOR?
DON'T DISAP-POINT SWORD!
COME ON, COME ON!!
LET'S GO!!
I'M SURE I CAN GET YOUR PARENTS' PERMIS-SION.
I'M A WELL-KNOWN RESEARCHER HERE IN GALAR.
VRROOM

UH-HUH... SURE, MOM... THANKS. TALK TO YOU LATER!
I CAN'T BELIEVE IT. SHE SAID I CAN GO...
YOU WON'T REGRET IT!
IT'S ALL THANKS TO YOU.
MY PARENTS WANTED TO KNOW HOW I MET THE AUTHORITY ON DYNAMAX RESEARCH!
PEOPLE THINK THE GALAR REGION'S POWER SPOTS ENABLE POKÉMON TO DYNAMAX AND BECOME GIGANTIC...
BUT IT'S NOT JUST THE LOCATION! MANY OTHER CONDITIONS ARE NEEDED FOR A POKÉMON TO GO DYNAMAX.
I HAD CASEY CREATE THE SIMULATOR TO HELP ME WITH MY RESEARCH.
BUT THAT'S NOT THE ONLY REASON I MADE IT!
WHAT DO YOU MEAN ...?

ISN'T IT OBVIOUS?! SO WE CAN TRAIN FOR OUR GYM CHALLENGES!
YOU'RE GOING TO CHALLENGE THE GYMS?!
WE WANT TO.
BUT IT'S DIFFICULT TO QUALIFY!
BAM BAM
WHERE I'M FROM, ANYONE CAN CHALLENGE A GYM AS LONG AS THEY'RE A TRAINER...
IN GALAR, YOU NEED A SKILLED TRAINER'S RECOMMEN-DATION TO QUALIFY FOR GYM CHALLENGES.
YOU CAN ALSO GET RECOMMENDA-TIONS FROM THE CHAMPION AND MEMBERS OF THE POKÉMON LEAGUE COMMITTEE.
WHO'S THE CHAMPION OF GALAR?

I THINK THERE'S A TV SPECIAL ON THE UP-COMING GYM CHALLENGES TONIGHT...
THE CHAMPION IS SCHEDULED TO APPEAR IN IT!
FIRST WE NEED TO MAKE SOME DINNER.
THERE'S TIME BEFORE THE SHOW STARTS IF WE HURRY!
THE CHALLENGE IS TO TRAVEL TO ALL EIGHT STADIUMS AND DEFEAT THEIR GYM LEADERS!
TRAINERS WHO PASS THE GYM CHALLENGE...
...MAY PARTICIPATE IN THE ANNUAL TOURNAMENT TO DETERMINE THE LEAGUE CHAMPION!
THE CHAMPION CUP!

AND NOW, I'LL INTRODUCE YOU TO OUR GUEST!
SINCE MAKING HIS DEBUT, THE CURRENT CHAMPION HASN'T LOST A SINGLE BATTLE...
SHAA
MEET LEON!
ABOUT THAT...
THE CHAMPION HASN'T ARRIVED IN WEDGEHURST YET?
IT SEEMS A GROUP OF WOOLOO HAVE WANDERED ONTO THE TRAIN TRACKS OUTSIDE WEDGEHURST...
...AND NOW THERE ARE DELAYS ON THE LINE...
THE TRACKS HEADING FOR MOTOSTOKE JUST OUTSIDE WEDGEHURST...
THAT'S CLOSE TO HERE!
THERE IT IS!

FOUND HIM!
A VIKAVOLT VIDEO DRONE!
WHAT IS THAT?!
RRRM!!
IT'S LEON!
A CHARI-ZARD?!
!
LOOK CLOSER!
HE'S BEING CHASED! WE SHOULD HELP HIM!

ROLL ROLL ROLL ROLL
THAT'S HOW THEY'RE GETTING THE WOOLOO AWAY FROM THE TRAIN TRACKS!
LEON IS LEADING THE WOOLOO, AND THE CHARIZARD IS HERDING THEM.
RRRMMBBLL
I WISH I KNEW WHAT'S DRAWING THE WOOLOO TO THE TRAIN TRACKS...
IT'S BEEN LIKE THIS FOR AGES, LEON.
ANOTHER GROUP HAS ESCAPED!
WHAT?!
NOT AGAIN!

AND YOU TWO ARE...?
THE PROBLEM ISN'T THE TRAIN TRACKS. IT'S WHAT'S INSIDE THE FENCE...
RIGHT?
...
I'M HENRY SWORD. AND WE'D LIKE TO HELP.
I'M CASEY SHIELD!
SWIP!
CASEY, I'LL BE COUNTING ON YOUR NAVIGATION.
GOT-CHA!
HENRY, ON YOUR LEFT! THERE'S A CLOUD OF SMOKE!
KEEP GOING!

GO RIGHT!
IT'S AN OBSTA-GOON!
THAT'S THE LAST OF THEM!
SO THAT POKÉMON WAS SCARING THE WOOLOO INSIDE THE FENCE!
SLAM!
WHAK!!

HE USED OB-STRUCT!
THE LEEK SPEAR DIDN'T AFFECT IT!
IN THAT CASE...
CONFUSE IT WITH YOUR QUICK STEPS!
LOOK!
IT CAN'T TELL WHICH ATTACK TO BLOCK!

DASH!!
SWAM!
ROLL ROLL
ALL CLEAR!

THANKS!
NO PROB-LEM!
YOU BETTER HURRY TO THE TV STATION! THERE'S STILL TIME!
PROFES-SOR MAGNO-LIA!
NICE TO SEE YOU AGAIN, LEON.
ARE THESE YOUR FRIENDS?
YES, THEY'RE HELPING ME WITH MY RESEARCH.
HOW'S SONIA DOING?
SHE'S BEEN BUSY TRAVELING.
PLEASE TELL HER SHE SHOULD COME SEE THE CHAMPION-SHIP CUP. IT STARTS NEXT WEEK.
OKAY! BUT YOU SHOULD HURRY NOW.

TOOOOOT
YEP!
PERFECT TIMING, PROFES-SOR!
THE PLAN WORKED!
NO BIGGIE.
PROFES-SOR, YOU KNOW THE CHAMPION?
BUT HE'LL REMEMBER HOW WE STEPPED UP TO HELP!
LEON WOULDN'T HAVE HAD ANY TROUBLE DEFEATING OBSTAGOON AND HERDING THE WOOLOO BY HIMSELF.
SQUEEE
WHAT DO YOU MEAN?

IT DOESN'T HURT THAT WE'RE PROFESSOR MAGNOLIA'S ASSISTANTS, EITHER!
AND WE DIDN'T JUST DEFEAT OBSTAGOON, WE STARED IT DOWN AND DROVE IT AWAY, SO WE PROBABLY SEEM MYSTERIOUS AND POWERFUL!
WHAT'S THAT?
HELLO, LEON.
CIAO...
I SEE. WELL, FIND OUT MORE ABOUT THEM AND LET ME KNOW.
IT'S BEEN A LONG TIME SINCE YOU'VE SOUNDED SO EXCITED...
A TRAINER YOU'D LIKE TO RECOMMEND?
I'LL GET RIGHT ON IT...
WELL, OLEANA?

CHAIRMAN ROSE.
WHAT? LEON DIDN'T SHOW UP?!
THE TRAIN SHOULD HAVE GOTTEN HIM THERE IN PLENTY OF TIME!
LEON'S ALWAYS HAD AN AWFUL SENSE OF DIRECTION...
HMM?
HOW DID I END UP BACK HERE?!

THE SECRETS OF DYNAMAX, PART 2

## Power Spots

A Pokémon needs to be in a Power Spot in order to Dynamax!

▲The Power Spot Detector is used to find Power Spots!

Adventure 3 Chomp!! Defeat Drednaw
NOD
NOD
WHERE AM I?
HMM?
OH YEAH!
I'M INSIDE PROFESSOR MAGNOLIA'S RV.
I'VE SET OUT ON MY POKÉMON JOURNEY.
PRO-FES-SOR?
HENRY? CASEY?
FOURTEEN SECONDS!
CASEY? IS THAT YOU?

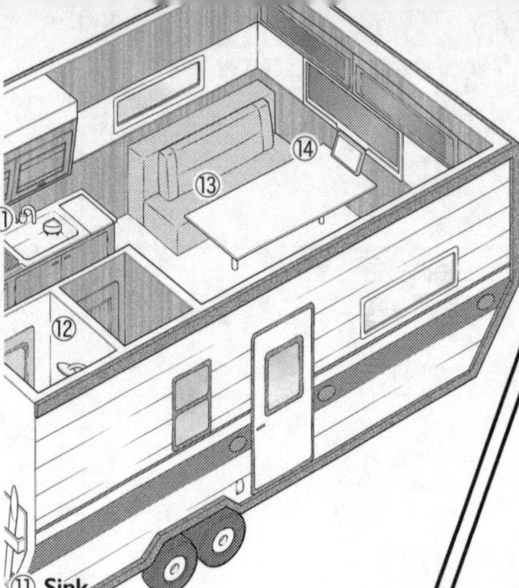


**⑪ Sink**

Shelf contains a big pot for campfire curry cookouts.

**⑫ Bathroom**

No rest stops needed! There's a shower and a toilet.

**⑬ Living room and bedroom**

Fold up the table and open out the sofa to create Shield and the professor's bed!

**⑭ TV**

THE COMPLETE FLOOR PLAN!

# INSIDE THE MAGNOLIA...

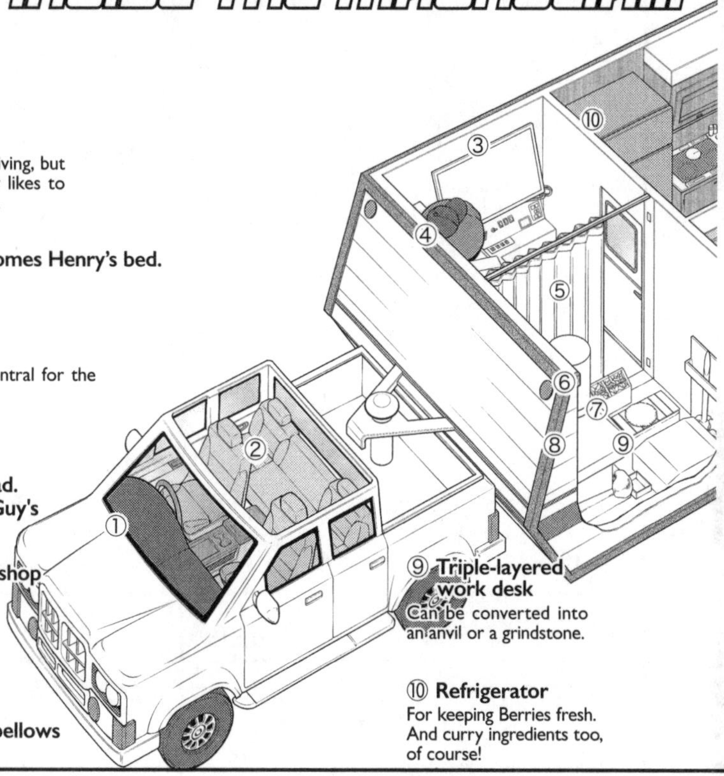

① **Tow truck**

The truck is self-driving, but the professor really likes to be behind the wheel.

② **The seat becomes Henry's bed.**

③ **Casey's lab**

This is command central for the Dynamax Simulator.

④ **Ball Guy's head. Is this the Ball Guy's real head?**

⑤ **Henry's workshop**

⑥ **Toolbox**

⑦ **Cushion**

⑧ **Furnace and bellows**

⑨ **Triple-layered work desk**

Can be converted into an anvil or a grindstone.

⑩ **Refrigerator**

For keeping Berries fresh. And curry ingredients too, of course!

SO WE SHOULD HAVE JUST RECORDED HIM DRIVING THE OBSTAGOON AWAY. BUT...
IT'S ALSO IMPORTANT TO GET HIM TO NOTICE US! WE WON'T GET ANYWHERE UNLESS WE GET PERMISSION TO TAKE PART IN THE GYM BATTLES!
WHERE IS PRO-FESSOR MAGNO-LIA?
DRIVING!
BUT SHE OUGHT TO LET THE TRUCK DRIVE ITSELF!
SHE'S ALWAYS LOVED TO DRIVE CARS...
...AND RACE ALONG MOUN-TAIN TRAILS.
CASEY, WOULD YOU MIND LOOKING AT THE DATA FOR SIRFETCH'D, TOO?
YOU BET!
THIS IS FROM WHEN IT SAVED MARVIN!
AND THIS IS FROM THE BATTLE WITH THE PANGORO PRO-GRAM!
SO NOW I CAN ANALYZE ITS MOVES FROM THE BATTLE AGAINST OSTAGOON...
...AND CREATE GRAPHICAL IMAGES TO MAKE IT EASY FOR US TO COMPARE...

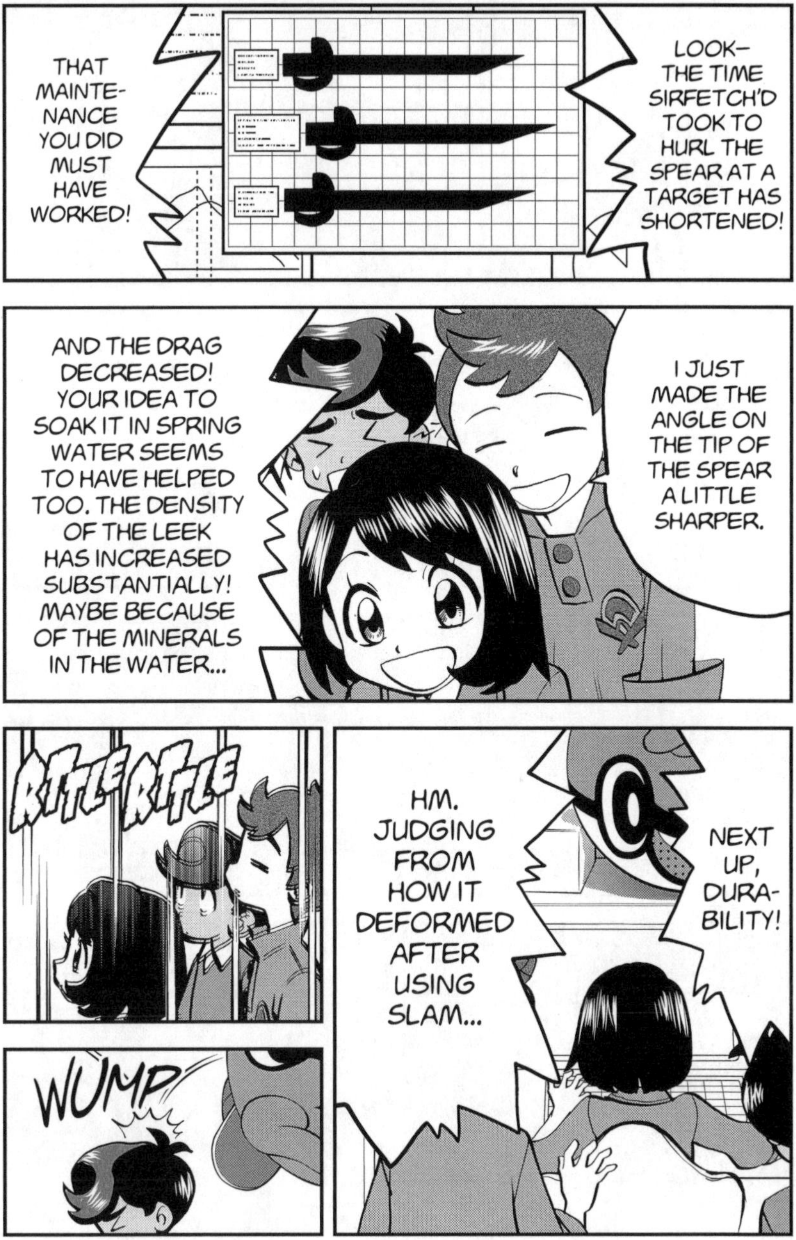
LOOK— THE TIME SIRFETCH'D TOOK TO HURL THE SPEAR AT A TARGET HAS SHORTENED!
THAT MAINTE-NANCE YOU DID MUST HAVE WORKED!
I JUST MADE THE ANGLE ON THE TIP OF THE SPEAR A LITTLE SHARPER.
AND THE DRAG DECREASED! YOUR IDEA TO SOAK IT IN SPRING WATER SEEMS TO HAVE HELPED TOO. THE DENSITY OF THE LEEK HAS INCREASED SUBSTANTIALLY! MAYBE BECAUSE OF THE MINERALS IN THE WATER...
NEXT UP, DURA-BILITY!
HM. JUDGING FROM HOW IT DEFORMED AFTER USING SLAM...
RATTLE RATTLE
WUMP

PROFESSOR, WHAT HAPPENED?
WE HAVE A FLAT TIRE.
I'LL TAKE A LOOK.
I'LL HELP TOO!
HOLD IT! YOU DON'T KNOW WHAT'S OUT THERE!
HUH?
A WILD POKÉMON COULD HAVE CAUSED THE FLAT!
SHUFF

KLAK
KLAK
COAST'S CLEAR!
THOK!
IT'S THIS TIRE. I'LL TAKE A LOOK AT THE PUNCTURE. COULD YOU GIVE US A LIGHT, SCOR-BUNNY?
HEY, SOBBLE, WHAT ARE YOU DOING OUTSIDE ?!
THE PUNCTURE WAS MADE BY RUNNING OVER SOMETHING HARD AND SHARP!

PLIP PLIP...
BUT SOBBLE DOESN'T HAVE A TRAINER YET!
IT WANTS TO HELP!
IF IT BUMPS INTO A STRONG WILD POKÉMON, IT WON'T KNOW HOW TO RUN AWAY OR FIGHT!
WAARGH
WHY ARE YOU CRYING?
YOU START-ED IT!
WHAT?

IT'S SOBBLE. ITS TEARS ARE SAID TO PACK THE CHEMICAL PUNCH OF A HUNDRED ONIONS.
SNIFF SNIFF... IS THAT SO.
SOBBLE, LET'S WAIT INSIDE THE TRUCK TOGETHER.
KRR SH
KRR SH
WHAT ?!
DON'T YOU WANT TO COME WITH ME?
I FEEL LIKE CRYING AGAIN.
BOOOSH

DRED-NAW! THREE OF THEM!
SHF
SHF
THE SHAPE OF THE PUNC-TURE MATCH-ES ITS SHELL!
WE MUST HAVE RUN OVER ONE!

MARVIN, GET INSIDE!
BYE!
WHOA!
RRCHOMP
LOOKS LIKE THEY'RE GONNA ATTACK.
SHIELD, WHAT KIND OF POKÉMON IS IT?
UH...
I DUNNO.
I'M SURE IT'S A DREDNAW...
...
BUT THE TYPE SLIPPED MY MIND!

TMP
TMP
THOK
TMP
TMP
TMP
SEPARATE THE THREE OF THEM!
SCOR-BUNNY!
MAYBE IT'LL COME TO ME WHILE WE'RE FIGHTING!
TMP
TMP
WHOMP!
TMP
TALK ABOUT HOT-FOOTING IT!
...ITS FEET ARE ON FIRE!
IT'S SO FAST...

BWO
RIGHT! THE PADS ON THE BACK OF ITS FEET ARE PRE-HEATED AND READY TO FIGHT!
GO!
GOODNESS GRACIOUS, DREDNAW'S ON FIRE!
SIZZLE
SIZZLE
SCOR-BUNNY, GET 'EM!

CLOMP
CLOMP
CLOMP
CLOMP
CLOMP
ZWOOSH
HENRY, CASEY IS IN TROU...
BUT HOW COULD IT CATCH UP WITH SCORBUNNY?!
KCH
OH NO! HENRY'S IN TROUBLE TOO!
KCH
KCH
KRCH

THEIR SMART-PHONES ARE INSIDE ON THE TABLE. GO GET THEM!
MARVIN!
WHAT IF I CAN'T THROW THEM FAR ENOUGH?
DON'T WORRY!
I dunno...
HUUH!
SWSSH
I DID MY BEST...

SHUP!
WHIZZ
WHAAAAAT?!
PRO-FES-SOR?
HAVE YOU HEARD OF THE POKÉMON CALLED ROTOM?
ROTOM IS A POKÉMON THAT LOVES TO ENTER ELECTRIC APPLIANCES LIKE VACUUM CLEANERS AND REFRIGERATORS...
...AND IN GALAR, WE PUT THEM IN OUR SMART-PHONES.

AND TONIGHT, I INSTALLED A POKÉDEX ON THEIR ROTOM PHONES.
A POKÉ-DEX!
THEN HENRY AND CASEY ARE...
...POKÉDEX HOLDERS!

Bite Pokémon
Type WATER ROCK
Height 3'03"
Weight 254.6 lbs
Number Battled 3
With jaws that can shear through steel rods, this highly aggressive Pokémon chomps down on its unfortunate prey.
Bite Pokémon
Type WATER ROCK
Height 3'03"
Weight 254.6 lbs
Number Battled 1
This Pokémon rapidly extends its retractable neck to sink its sharp fangs into distant enemies and take them down.
YOU STRENGTHENED GROOKEY'S STICK, BUT BE CAREFUL–DREDNAW MIGHT CHOMP IT!
CASEY, STAY AWAY! IT'S GOT A LONG REACH!
GROOKEY, LET GO OF YOUR STICK!
YOU'LL NEVER YANK IT FREE OF DRED-NAW'S JAWS!
IT'LL BE OKAY! I CAN FIX IT AFTER THE BATTLE!

BUOSH
SHF
SHF SHF SHF
THE BURNED DREDNAW IS SLOWING DOWN! KEEP IT BUSY WHILE IT WEARS ITSELF OUT!
GTSI
OH NO, SCOR-BUNNY!
KRBRRN
IT BIT ITS FLAME POUCH!
CHM

SOBBLE, WHERE'D YOU COME FROM?
OH NO...
WHAT'S A FLAME POUCH?
AN ORGAN FOR FIRE, LIKE A SECOND HEART.
GRRRR..
LOOK OUT!
CLOMP
CLOMP
CLOMP
FWOOM
FWOOM
FWOO
FWOO

SPLOOSH
SOBBLE DISAP-PEARED ?!
ZHEEN
STAGGER
STAGGER
THUMP

GROOKEY, NOW!
THUNGK!!
WHERE DID SOBBLE GO?!
SOBBLE BECOMES INVISIBLE WHEN IT GETS WET.
UM...
IT'S RIGHT HERE.
FWOO
FWOO
FWOOOM

IF YOU AND SOBBLE AGREE, THERE'S NOTHING TO STOP YOU!
ME ?!
RE-ALLY ?!
MARVIN, WOULD YOU LIKE TO TAKE CARE OF SOBBLE?
...
WHAT DO YOU THINK, SOBBLE?
BMP
BMP

VRROOM
TURF-FIELD STADIUM
MILO! MILO!
MEANWHILE, AT TURF-FIELD...
IT'S NOT LIKE HIM TO DO THAT.
LEON RECOM-MENDED TWO TRAINERS FOR THE GYM CHALLENGE, RIGHT?
TURFFIELD STADIUM GYM LEADER: MILO
DID YOU HEAR ?!
LEON!
YEAH, I HEARD.

THE CHAMPION RECOMMENDED A CHALLENGER? TWO OF THEM?
HULBURY STADIUM GYM LEADER: NESSA
REGARDLESS OF WHOEVER RECOMMENDED THEM, I WILL FIGHT THEM WITH EVERYTHING I'VE GOT LIKE I ALWAYS DO.
MOTOSTOKE STADIUM GYM LEADER: KABU
HOW INTER-ESTING.
BALLONLEA STADIUM GYM LEADER: OPAL
THE NEWS OF THE UN-DEFEATED CHAMPION, LEON, RECOM-MENDING NEW CHALLENG-ERS...
...QUICKLY TRAVELED THROUGH THE STADIUMS OF GALAR.

THE SECRETS OF DYNAMAX, PART 3

▲ A pillar of red light emanates from a Power Spot in the Wild Area.

**Wild Area**

The Wild Area is known to have many Power Spots. Inhabited by countless Pokémon, anyone who comes near a Power Spot risks a Dynamax battle.

THE SOB.
HIS SOBBLENESS.
EL SOBBERINO...
NO, THAT'S TOO LONG.
MORNING!
WHAT ARE YOU TWO DOING?
GOOD MORNING, CASEY.
HENRY AND I WERE COMING UP WITH NICKNAMES FOR SOBBLE.
ONCE WE START HAVING GYM BATTLES, WE'LL MEET MANY OTHER TRAINERS.
GROOKEY, SCRATCH!
GROOKEY, BRANCH POKE!
?!
IT MIGHT BE CONFUSING WHEN WE END UP FACING A TRAINER WITH THE SAME KIND OF POKÉMON.
Happens all the time, right?
AND HAVE YOU DECIDED ON NAMES?

## A Rising Beam of Light

YOU'RE SNIFFLER!
I KNOW!
WE'RE HERE!
WE'RE WHERE?!
THE WILD AREA, OF COURSE!
Adventure 4 Zap!!

OH WOW!
IT'S A PRISTINE WILDERNESS FULL OF WILD POKÉMON.
WHAT'S THE WILD AREA...?
YOU ARE FREE TO TRAIN AND CAPTURE NEW POKÉMON HERE.
BUT YOU COULD RUN INTO SOME EXTREMELY STRONG POKÉMON...
...SO YOU NEED TO BE CARE-FUL.
CASEY, LET'S START OUR INVESTIGA-TION FROM THE ROLLING FIELDS.
YOU BET!
SO HER RESEARCH INTO DYNAMAX BRINGS HER HERE...
...TO THE WILD AREA?
INVESTI-GATION?
OF COURSE! WE'RE HERE BECAUSE OF PRO-FESSOR MAGNOLIA'S RESEARCH!

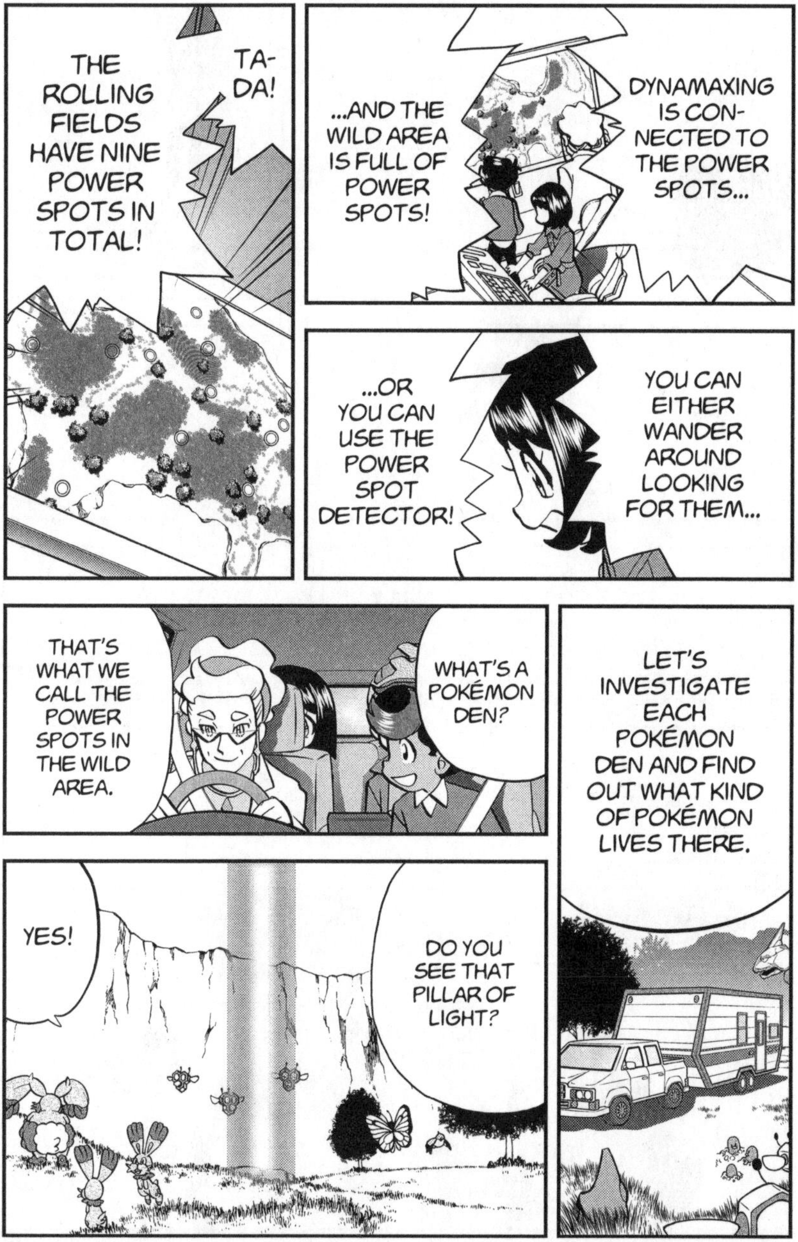
THE ROLLING FIELDS HAVE NINE POWER SPOTS IN TOTAL!
TA-DA!
...AND THE WILD AREA IS FULL OF POWER SPOTS!
DYNAMAXING IS CON-NECTED TO THE POWER SPOTS...
YOU CAN EITHER WANDER AROUND LOOKING FOR THEM...
...OR YOU CAN USE THE POWER SPOT DETECTOR!
THAT'S WHAT WE CALL THE POWER SPOTS IN THE WILD AREA.
WHAT'S A POKÉMON DEN?
LET'S INVESTIGATE EACH POKÉMON DEN AND FIND OUT WHAT KIND OF POKÉMON LIVES THERE.
YES!
DO YOU SEE THAT PILLAR OF LIGHT?

A POKÉMON LITERALLY LIVES INSIDE IT.
BELOW THAT LIGHT...
...WILL BE A DYNAMAXED POKÉMON.
THAT'S A REAL DYNAMAXED POKÉMON!
GULP
NOT A VR ONE LIKE I SAW YESTERDAY!
ENTERING A DEN MEANS WE'LL HAVE TO FIGHT THAT POKÉMON!
AND IF WE WIN, WE CAN CAPTURE IT!
THAT'S A BIG IF!
AS FOR TODAY, WE CAME HERE TO GATHER DATA.
PLEASE DON'T IMMEDIATELY CHARGE INTO THE DENS.
IS THERE ANY WAY TO KNOW WHAT SORT OF POKÉMON IS IN THE DEN?
THE APP IN OUR ROTOM PHONE WILL TELL US IF WE GET CLOSE ENOUGH!
DING! ♪

OVER HERE!
MAIL!
FLAP
FLAP
FLAP
THANK YOU!
I LOVE GETTING MAIL!
CASEY SH
THANKS!
TMP!

HEY, IT'S FROM THE GYM CHALLENGE OFFICE!
TA-DA!
UNI-FORMS?
OFFICIAL UNI-FORMS! OUR CHAL-LENGE BANDS WERE INSIDE TOO!
I GUESS THAT MEANS WE'RE OFFICIAL!
OFFICIAL PARTICI-PANTS WEAR THE UNIFORM FOR GYM BATTLES.
IS THERE A MEANING BEHIND THE UNIFORM NUMBER?
I LOVE PALIN-DROMES. ♡
808
303

LET'S TRY THEM ON AND SEE IF THEY FIT!
GOOD IDEA!
WHOA! WHOA!
USH!!
USH!!
HEY!
BE CAREFUL! YOU MIGHT RIP IT!
RIP IT?!
YOU'LL RIP YOUR LIP IF YOU KEEP YAPPIN'!
JUST GIVE UP NOW!
YOU'LL NEVER WIN YOUR GYM CHAL-LENGE, HENRY SWORD AND CASEY SHIELD!
WHAT ARE YOU TALKING ABOUT?!

HOW DO YOU KNOW WHO WE ARE?
TWO YOUNG TRAINERS RECOMMENDED BY THE CHAMP HIMSELF...
...SAID TO BE TRAVELIN' WITH PROFESSOR MAGNOLIA IN AN RV!
IT'S THE BIGGEST NEWS IN GALAR!
THAT'S WHY WE'RE HERE TO STOP YOU!
WE'RE TEAM YELL!
YOU'RE TRYING TO STOP US FROM CARRYING OUT OUR GYM CHALLENGE?!
THAT'S RIGHT!
DO IT, LINOONE!
GO, THIEVUL!

SUCKER PUNCH!
VRRK!
LANCE-LOT!
NIGHT SLASH!
WHAT IS YOUR PROBLEM?!
SLISSH
TEAM YELL MAKES SURE OUR PRINCESS WINS!
WHAT PRIN-CESS?!

BOW BEFORE OUR PRINCESS! THE ONE AND ONLY...
...MARNIE!!
YOU EXPECT ME TO BELIEVE A PRINCESS TOLD YOU TO COME BULLY US?!
GASP!
MARNIE WOULD NEVER TELL US TO DO SOMETHING SO WRONG!
SUCH DISRE-SPECT!
SO YOU KNOW THIS IS WRONG!

WE FORBID YOUR SUCCESS!
WE MUST ENSURE MARNIE'S VICTORY!
SCOR-BUNNY!
THIS CONVER-SATION IS ABSURD!
ONCE MORE!
LINOONE HAS BEEN BURNED!
SHFF

SHA
THUNGK
THAT LINOONE HAS QUICK FEET, A HIDDEN ABILITY!
ITS SPEED INCREASED BECAUSE IT HAS A STATUS CONDITION!
NO WAY!
...
TWIGGY ...
PSST, PSST.

YOU'RE NOT ALLOWED TO ATTACK THE TRAINER!
AIYEEE!
OW!
THK
THK
OKAY!
CASEY, TAKE THIS.
KLIK!
KLIK!
WOO!
CUT IT OUT!
HEY!
THK
GSH

SHWOOM!
THEY DISAP-PEARED!
HENRY, CASEY, TEAM YELL AND THEIR POKÉMON TOO!
WHAT'S GOING ON?
WHAT WILL THEY HAVE TO BATTLE?!
RR
MM...
RRM BB...
RRM BB BL L

SO THIS IS A DEN, HUH?
IT'S HUGE!
AHHH!
HOW DARE YOU DRAG US DOWN HERE!
WE CAN'T GET OUT UNLESS WE FIGHT THAT DYNAMAXED GURDURR!
THAT'S RIGHT.

WE'LL HAVE TO FIGHT TO-GETHER.
GRRR ...!
GWOOO
WHUMP
AIYEEEE!
IT FLAT-TENED LINOONE WITH ONE HIT!
MY TURN!
THIEVUL, FIRE FANG!

CHOMP!
GLOMP!
KRRSH!
THAT ONLY MADE THINGS WORSE. I GUESS ITS ABILITY IS GUTS.
HOW ARE YOU SO CALM ?!
USE FIRE FANG AGAIN!
BUT THIS TIME, ATTACK ITS GEAR, THE STEEL BEAM.
YOU TOO, SHIELD.
SCOR-BUNNY, EMBER!
SURE THING!
CHOOM
CHOOM
CHOOM
CHOOM
CHOOM

SHWAAA
SHFF
THUNGKT!!
KEEP HEATING THE STEEL BEAM WITH SCORBUNNY'S FIRE!
KEEP ATTACKING, CASEY!
THIEVUL HAS BEEN DEFEAT-ED!

GRRRGH!
FWOOSH
SIZZLE
SIZZLE
THE STEEL BEAM'S HEATIN' UP!
EXACT-LY.
NOW, LANCE-LOT!
USE BRAVE BIRD!
SNAP!

KRR-THONCK!!
FWUMP!
KCH
KRCH
KRCH
GOOD!

TMP
LET'S DO IT!
SHOOOOM
KLIKT
THU NGK

NOW POCKET-SIZE!
GURDURR.
OH, GROSS!
THANK YOU VERY MUCH FOR YOUR HELP.
I THINK I'LL CALL HIM STEELER.
WHAT'LL YOU CALL IT?
I MANAGED TO CAPTURE A GURDURR! I'VE ALWAYS WANTED ONE!
YOU SURE HANDLED THOSE GOONS, AND...
WAY TO GO, HENRY!

YOU KNEW THERE WAS A GURDURR INSIDE THE DEN?
MY APP TOLD ME.
HMPH...
I THOUGHT I TOLD YOU NOT TO JUMP INSIDE THE DEN...
BUT SINCE YOU MANAGED TO CAPTURE GURDURR, THAT MEANS THE DYNAMAX BAND WORKED.
YEP!
LIKE A DREAM!
UM... WHAT IS THE DYNAMAX BAND?
SINCE YOU'RE A MEMBER OF OUR TEAM NOW...
...I THINK IT'S TIME I TOLD YOU ABOUT EVERYTHING.

## THE SECRETS OF DYNAMAX, PART 4

▲ Pluck up the courage to jump inside and battle a giant!

### Den

A pillar of red light means you've found a Pokémon Den! A powerful Dynamaxed Pokémon will be waiting for you inside!

**Hidenori Kusaka** is the writer for *Pokémon Adventures*. Running continuously for over 20 years, *Pokémon Adventures* is the only manga series to completely cover all the *Pokémon* games and has become one of the most popular series of all time. In addition to writing manga, he also edits children's books and plans mixed-media projects for Shogakukan's children's magazines. He uses the Pokémon Electrode as his author portrait.

---

**Satoshi Yamamoto** is the artist for *Pokémon Adventures*, which he began working on in 2001, starting with volume 10. Yamamoto launched his manga career in 1993 with the horror-action title *Kimen Senshi*, which ran in Shogakukan's *Weekly Shonen Sunday* magazine, followed by the series *Kaze no Denshosha*. Yamamoto's favorite manga creators/artists include Fujiko Fujio (*Doraemon*), Yukinobu Hoshino (*2001 Nights*) and Katsuhiro Otomo (*Akira*). He loves films, monsters, detective novels and punk rock music. He uses the Pokémon Swalot as his artist portrait.

**Pokémon: Sword & Shield**
**Volume 1**
**VIZ Media Edition**

Story by HIDENORI KUSAKA
Art by SATOSHI YAMAMOTO

©2021 Pokémon.
©1995–2020 Nintendo / Creatures Inc. / GAME FREAK inc.
TM, ®, and character names are trademarks of Nintendo.
© 2020 Hidenori KUSAKA, Satoshi YAMAMOTO
All rights reserved.
Original Japanese edition published by SHOGAKUKAN.
English translation rights in the United States of America, Canada, the United Kingdom, Ireland, Australia and New Zealand arranged with SHOGAKUKAN.

**Original Cover Design**—Hiroyuki KAWASOME (grafio)

**Translation**—Tetsuichiro Miyaki
**English Adaptation**—Molly Tanzer
**Touch-Up & Lettering**—Annaliese "Ace" Christman
**Design**—Alice Lewis
**Editor**—Joel Enos

The stories, characters and incidents mentioned in this publication are entirely fictional.

No portion of this book may be reproduced or transmitted in any form or by any means without written permission from the copyright holders.

Printed in the U.S.A.

Published by VIZ Media, LLC
P.O. Box 77010
San Francisco, CA 94107

10 9 8 7 6 5 4 3
First printing, August 2021
Third printing, May 2024

ratings.viz.com
RATED A ALL AGES

**PARENTAL ADVISORY**
POKÉMON: SWORD & SHIELD is rated A and is suitable for readers of all ages.

VIZ MEDIA
viz.com

# Coming Next Volume

## Volume 2

Henry, Casey and their friends arrive at Motostoke to participate in the Gym Challenge. They've missed the opening ceremonies, but they're still able to join in the challenges! Henry's first official battle pits him against Gym Leader Milo.

Will Henry's first Dynamax battle also be his last?!

## THIS IS THE END OF THIS GRAPHIC NOVEL!

To properly enjoy this VIZ Media graphic novel, please turn it around and begin reading from right to left.

This book has been printed in the original Japanese format in order to preserve the orientation of the original artwork. Have fun with it!

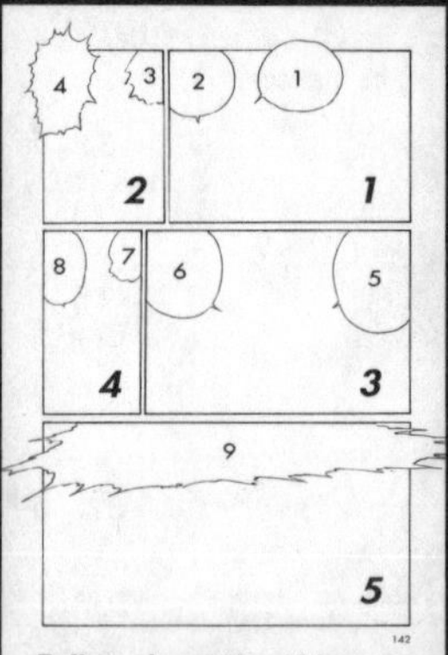

**Follow the action this way.**